JUST ONE QUICK

KICK

Center for Responsive Schools, Inc., is a not-for-profit educational organization.

© 2023 by Fly Five: The Social and Emotional Learning Curriculum

First edition, April 2023
10 9 8 7 6 5 4 3 2 1

This book is part of the Adventures of the Center City Kids series.

Fly Five Team:
Jazmine Franklin, Chief Program Officer
Anjail Kenyatta, Director of Content and Curriculum Development
Samantha Nacht, Creative and Art Director
Ellie Cornecelli, Director of Professional Development and Engagement
Janessa Martin, Curriculum and Instructional Designer
Najah Hijazi, Curriculum and Instructional Designer
Angelica Williams, Digital and Graphic Designer
Clay Caricofe, Graphic Designer
Josh Frederick, Graphic Designer
Negene Cord-Cruz, Graphic Designer
Hannah Shearer, Graphic Design Specialist

Contributing Writers: Rebecca Crutchfield, Savannah Elliott, Anjail Kenyatta, Amy Martin, Janessa Martin, Amanda Millard

Contributing Illustrators: Christina Dill, Samantha Jo, Kenny Kiernan, Lauren Scott, Kaitlyn Terrey, Ernon Wright

Concept Illustrator: Monika Suska

ISBN: 978-1-950317-31-8
Library of Congress Control Number: 2023931468
Printed in China

Avenue A Books
An imprint of
Fly Five: The Social and Emotional Learning Curriculum
85 Avenue A, P.O. Box 718
Turners Falls, MA 01376-0718
800-360-6332
flyfivesel.org

This book is dedicated to the honest mistakes we make . . . and those who forgive us for them!

Last night, I couldn't sleep.
I had a case of the jumpy jiggles.
Right before bed, my dad told me his
sister, my Auntie Abena, was coming
to visit all the way from Ghana,
a country in West Africa.

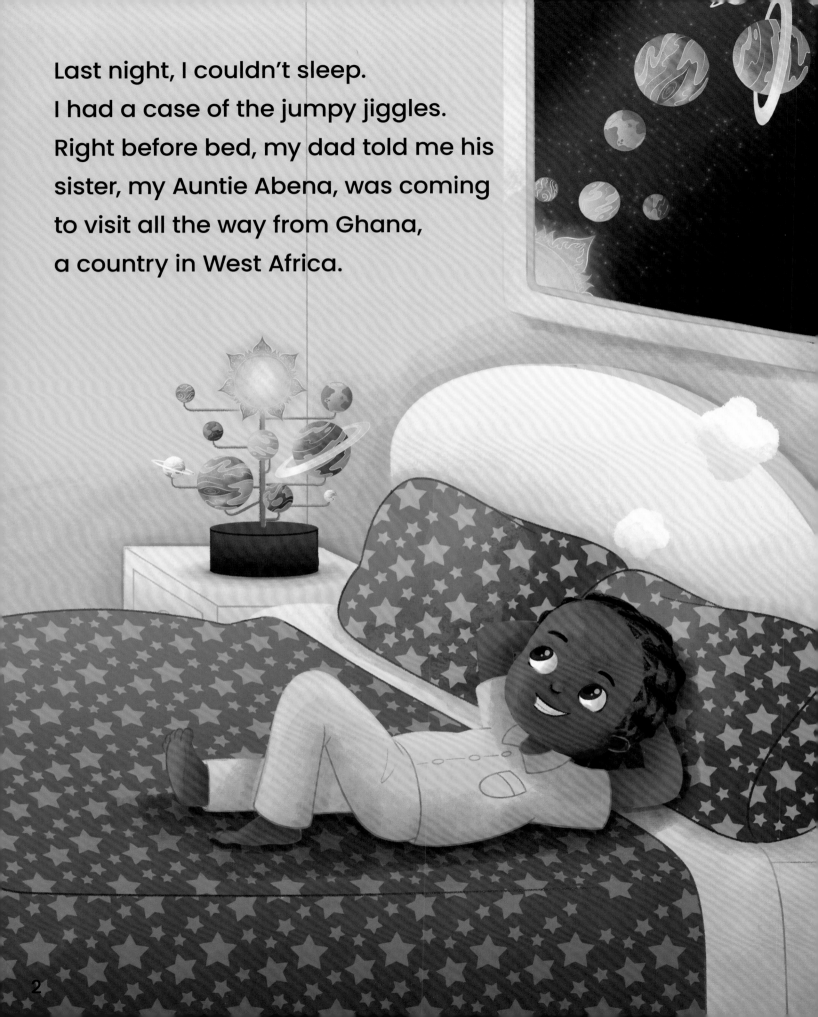

I love my Auntie Abena.
She's fun and she always brings me gifts.

Once, she brought me a poster of Ghana's soccer team, the Golden Champions. It was signed by the team's star player!

Another time, she brought me an official Golden Champions soccer jersey!

My mind was racing. . .

What will she have for me this time?

How long does it take to get here from Ghana?

When will she arrive?

Today is the day.
My auntie is here!
I run down the stairs
and jump straight into her arms.
She greets me with hugs and smiles.

6

Still holding my hand, she pulls me over to a colorful bag.

I know it's for me!

I open the bag.
Inside is a brand new
soccer ball. It is signed
by the same Golden
Champions player who
already signed my poster!

8

"Thank you!" I say as I gave my auntie a big hug.
"This is the **BEST GIFT EVER!**"

I am so excited. I want to try out my new soccer ball.
The jumpy jiggles are back!

I turn to my dad. "Dad, can we go play?"
I can already see myself kicking downfield
and scoring a goal.

Dad laughs. "Later, yes! It's raining now,
and I want to visit with your auntie."
Then he reminds me,

"NO SOCCER PLAYING IN THE HOUSE!"

"I won't, Dad," I promise. I know the rule.

Auntie brought my mom a gift also—a beautiful vase.
It was made by an artist in Ghana.
My auntie tells us what each color of the vase means—
yellow represents weath and royalty, and *green*
represents the country's rich forest.

"OOOOOH"

Mom loves the vase. She oooohs and aaaahs.
She puts it on a table in the living room.
"I want everyone to see it," she says.

The grown-ups go into the kitchen to talk.

I stay in the living room, holding my new soccer ball.

I put it on the floor.

I roll it under my feet so I can see how it feels.

IT FEELS JUST RIGHT!

I look outside.

Maybe it has cleared up?

NO! IT IS STILL RAINING.

I decide to see if I can *gently* kick the ball.

I'm not *playing* soccer. This is more like an experiment, which I do all the time with my science kit.

16

SCORE!

I gently kick the ball. It bounces across the living room, past Mom's green plant.

I do this a few times. Then I decide to try a *little* bit of dribbling so I can get the feel of my new ball. Dribbling is when you kick the ball back and forth to yourself.

The dribbling works fine until . . .

the ball gets out of control!

I try to steer it away with one quick kick,
but I somehow kick it **too** hard.

The ball flies in the air.

I run after it. I try to grab it.

But I am too late.

It hits my mom's new vase.

The vase falls on the floor with a

CRASH

and breaks into pieces.

What should I do? What can I say?

I didn't mean to break the vase!

Maybe I could glue it back together?
No, it's in so many pieces!
Maybe I could hide it? No, that won't work.
Everyone will wonder where it went.

My eyes fill with tears.
Auntie brought my mom an awesome gift
and I broke it. I also broke the house rule.
Everyone will be VERY, VERY, VERY mad.

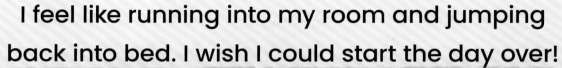

I feel like running into my room and jumping back into bed. I wish I could start the day over!

But I know I can't.

I slowly stand up.

22

After hearing the crash, Mom, Dad, and Auntie
come into the living room.
They look down at the broken vase.

I gulp.

"What happened, Kofi?" Dad asks.

At first, my mouth doesn't work. I open it,
but no words come out. I swallow and try again.
"I . . . I accidentally broke Mom's vase.
I'm so sorry, Mom! And Auntie! I wish I could fix it."

Mom isn't happy. Her eyes narrow.
But she kneels down beside me
and puts her arm around my shoulder.

She asks quietly, "How did you break it, Kofi?"

I look at Dad, then back at Mom.
"I was trying to gently dribble
my new soccer ball
and it got out of control.

I tried to kick it away
from your plant.

But I accidentally hit
the vase." My head
is down and my
voice is small.

27

My auntie crouches down beside
me and takes my hand.
"I accept your apology, dear Kofi.
And I appreciate your honesty."

She looks at the pieces all over the floor.
"This vase now has a new musical rhythm,"
she says with a chuckle.

She tells my mom she will bring her an
even more beautiful vase on the next visit.

"I accept your apology as well, Kofi," Mom adds.
"Your feelings seem genuine. I can see that you are
truly sorry. And I think that you owe your dad
an apology too."

"I'm sorry, Dad.
I broke my promise not to play soccer in the house."

My dad looks into my eyes.
"Kofi, rules help us make the right decisions.
Rules keep everyone safe.
And rules help us respect others and their property.
Do you understand?"

I nodded my head yes.

"Kofi, I appreciate your openness and honesty in telling us what happened," says my dad. "So, I, too, accept your apology."

Then my dad hugs me tightly.

I feel so much better now that I told the truth. I start to smile a little. Then, I offer to sweep up the broken vase.

My auntie suggests that she and I can use
the bigger pieces to make an art project this afternoon.

"Mom will love this!" I say.
"A mosaic stone for her garden."

Adventures of the Center City Kids

Adventures of the Center City Kids is a collection of engaging, relevant, and relatable books for children and youth that promote literacy skills, celebrate family, and amplify cultural diversity. This series supports academic, social, and emotional growth in five core competencies: cooperation, assertiveness, responsibility, empathy, and self-control. The Adventures of the Center City Kids series inspires readers to create a good life for themselves, their families, and their community.

🤝 Cooperation

An engaging book series about the ability to establish and maintain new relationships, resolve conflicts, and be a contributing member of the classroom and community.

👆 Assertiveness

An engaging book series about how to stand up for one's ideas without hurting or negating others, how to seek help, and how to persevere with a challenging task.

 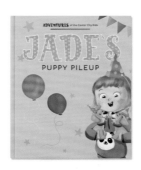  

AVENUE **a** BOOKS

Order the entire collection at flyfivesel.org

 Responsibility

An engaging book series about the ability to motivate oneself to act and follow through on expectations and the ability to define a problem, consider the consequences, and choose a positive solution.

 Empathy

An engaging book series about the ability to recognize one's emotions and be receptive to new ideas and perspectives.

Self-Control

An engaging book series about the ability to recognize and regulate one's thoughts, emotions, and behaviors in order to be successful in the moment and remain on a successful trajectory.

  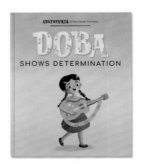 

CENTER CITY

1. Look at the map and locate Kofi's home. What are some nearby places he could visit?

2. Where do you think Kofi practices soccer? Why?

3. Where can Kofi and his family take Auntie Abena to explore?

Restaurants   Bakery

Hope Elementary School

Skate Park

Park

Soccer Field

Baseball Field

Convenience Store

Farmer's Market

Center for Performing

Gym

Bus Stop

Mindful Middle

Library

Groce